lore H

1979 September

from Mummy

P9-BYK-150

JUST THINK!

Alfred A. Knopf ☙ New York

JUST THINK!

by Betty Miles and Joan Blos
illustrated by Pat Grant Porter

For each other's families
JB & BM

For my father
PGP

This is a Borzoi Book
Published by Alfred A. Knopf, Inc.

Copyright © 1971 by Betty Miles and Joan Blos
Illustrations © 1971 by Pat Porter

All rights reserved under International and Pan-American Copyright Conventions.
Published in the United States by Alfred A. Knopf, Inc., New York,
and simultaneously in Canada by Random House of Canada Limited, Toronto.
Distributed by Random House, Inc., New York.

Trade Edition: ISBN: 0–394–82290–0
Library Edition: ISBN: 0–394–92290–5
Library of Congress Catalog Card Number: 77–151848

Reprinted by permission
''I Can Read'' from the Bank Street College Series
GREEN LIGHT, GO, copyright © 1966 The Macmillan Company, New York
Collier-Macmillan Canada, Ltd., Toronto, Ontario.

Manufactured in the United States of America

First Edition

Sources
Traditional: ''Infinity''
          ''Say It Fast''
          ''Feeling Good''
From The New-England Primer, 1727:
          ''Poems from a Very Old Book for American Children''

CONTENTS

THE LUCKY DAY

I found a penny!

I put my penny in the gum machine.
A blue gum came out.
And a ring came out, too!
A gold ring, with a red stone.

That was my lucky day.
I wonder when I'll be lucky again.

Maybe tomorrow?

YESTERDAY, TODAY, TOMORROW

Just think . . .
Yesterday is what you remember.
Today is now.
Tomorrow is what you sleep for.

Today
will be yesterday
tomorrow.

AN ALPHABET OF NAMES

Anthony
Barbara   **C**armen
Donna   **E**ugene
Felicia
George
Helen
Irving
Jessica
Karen
Lewis
Mary
Norman
Oscar
Pearl
Quentin
Rosalie
Sandra
Tom
Ursula
Vera
Walter
Xavier   **Y**oshiko
Zachary

THE SWEATER

On Sunday, the boy's grandmother began to knit.

SUNDAY
1
SEPTEMBER

Monday: she made a front.

MONDAY
2
SEPTEMBER

Thursday: she made another sleeve.

THURSDAY
5
SEPTEMBER

Friday: she sewed the parts together.

FRIDAY
6
SEPTEMBER

Tuesday: she made a back.

TUESDAY

3

SEPTEMBER

Wednesday:
she made one sleeve.

WEDNESDAY

4

SEPTEMBER

Saturday: she pressed it.

SATURDAY

7

SEPTEMBER

And on Sunday, the boy
wore his new sweater.

SUNDAY

8

SEPTEMBER

FALL

HIGH RISE

Just think . . .

Your ceiling
may be somebody else's floor.

Your floor
may be somebody else's ceiling.

Their ceiling may be somebody else's floor.
Their floor may be somebody else's ceiling.

Et cetera.

ON and ON and ON

A boy looking
at a picture of a boy looking
at a picture of a boy looking
at a picture of a boy looking . . .

I CAN
READ

I used to get hit by the door
That opens itself at the store.
I used to begin
To go OUT to get IN—
But I do not do that anymore.

I can read!

EVERYBODY

Just think . . .
Everybody in this picture
was a baby once.

Everybody in this picture
will be grown up some day.

SOME INTERESTING WORDS

CHANGES

Just think . . .   Batter turns into cake.

 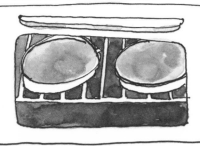 

A caterpillar becomes a butterfly.

Water freezes to ice.   New shoes get to be old shoes.

Night turns to day.   Day turns to night.   Night becomes day again.

And things keep on changing.

WINTER

INFINITY

Big Sky Ranch,
R.F.D. #3,
Kalispell,
Montana,
59901,
U.S.A.,
North America,
Western Hemisphere,
The World,
Space,
Solar System,
Our Galaxy,
The Universe . . .

Star bright,
Space light,
First star I see tonight,
I wish I may,
I wish I might,
Have the wish
I wish tonight.

Just think . . .
The world is like a spaceship.
It turns in space
And we ride on it.
All people ride together
On Spaceship Earth.

A BUSY DAY

WORDS THAT SOUND LIKE WHAT THEY MEAN

POW!

BAM!

SOCK!

THWACK!

PUSSY WILLOW

whisper

Shhhhhhhhhhhhhhhhhhhhhhhhhhhhhhhhhhhhhhhhhhhhhhhhhhhhhhhhhhhhhhhhhh

POEMS FROM
A VERY OLD BOOK
FOR AMERICAN CHILDREN
1727

The moon gives light
In time of night.

Nightingales sing
In time of spring.

My book and heart
Shall never part.

SPRING

A PARTY

One cookie
plus one cookie,
plus one cookie,
and something to drink
makes a party.

SEEING THINGS

Just think . . .
Things are how you see them:
With a magnifying glass—big.
In a mirror—backwards.
Through sunglasses—dark.
When you love them, lovely.

THE KITE

flew up

The kite

up

and away!

SAY IT FAST

Three gray geese
in the green grass grazing.

Three gray geese in the green grass grazing.

Threegraygeeseinthegreengrassgrazing!

THINGS THAT GO TOGETHER

Thunder and lightning go together.
So do hands and mittens,

Beans and rice, fire and ice,
Mother cats and kittens.

News and weather go together.
So do reading and writing,
Fish and bones!
Ice cream and cones!
Also, loving and fighting.

SUMMER

FEELING GOOD

I'll tell you the truth—
Don't think I'm lying:
I have to run backwards
To keep from flying!